MAX & MO's
Halloween Surprise

For another set of best friends,
Max and Mia —P. L.

For Patricia Lakin, with thanks —B. F.

ALADDIN PAPERBACKS
AN IMPRINT OF SIMON & SCHUSTER CHILDREN'S PUBLISHING DIVISION
1230 AVENUE OF THE AMERICAS, NEW YORK, NY 10020
TEXT COPYRIGHT © 2008 BY PATRICIA LAKIN
ILLUSTRATIONS COPYRIGHT © 2008 BY BRIAN FLOCA
ALL RIGHTS RESERVED, INCLUDING THE RIGHT OF REPRODUCTION IN WHOLE
OR IN PART IN ANY FORM.
READY-TO-READ IS A REGISTERED TRADEMARK OF SIMON & SCHUSTER, INC.
ALADDIN PAPERBACKS AND RELATED LOGO ARE REGISTERED TRADEMARKS
OF SIMON & SCHUSTER, INC.
DESIGNED BY LISA VEGA
THE TEXT OF THIS BOOK WAS SET IN CENTURY OLDSTYLE BT.
MANUFACTURED IN THE UNITED STATES OF AMERICA
FIRST ALADDIN PAPERBACKS EDITION AUGUST 2008
2 4 6 8 10 9 7 5 3 1
CATALOGING-IN-PUBLICATION DATA IS ON FILE WITH THE LIBRARY OF CONGRESS.
ISBN-13: 978-1-4169-2539-2
ISBN-10: 1-4169-2539-2

MAX & MO's
Halloween Surprise

By Patricia Lakin
Illustrated by Brian Floca

Ready-to-Read · Aladdin
New York London Toronto Sydney

Max and Mo
were best friends.

They lived in a school . . .
in the art room . . .
in a cozy cage.

Max liked to make things.

Mo liked to read things.

"I am reading that paper,"
said Mo.

"But I am making a chain,"
said Max.

"No more chains!"
said Mo.

"What can I make?"
asked Max.
"What can I read?"
asked Mo.

"Time to get out,"
said Mo.
"How?" asked Max.
"We jump!" said Mo.

Max scratched his ears.
"Now what?" he asked.
Mo scratched his chin.
"The chains!" he said.

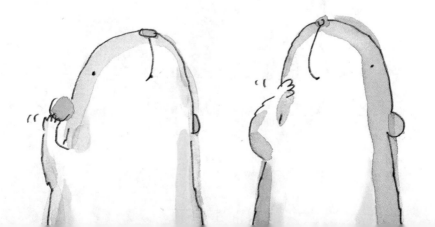

Max pulled them down.
Mo piled them up.
They climbed on top.
"One, two, three, jump!"

"Wheeeeee!"

"Cats and ghosts!"
said Max.

"They are not real,"
said Mo.
He read the sign.

"I want to make one, too,"
said Max.
"But how?"

Mo scratched his chin.
"Use these!"

Max scratched his ears.
"And these?"

Max took the plate.

He dipped his paw in paint.

He painted a cat face.

He put on his mask.

"Help!" said Max.

"Where are you?"

"Cut out eye holes,"
Mo read.

"I will cut this, too."

Max held up a white cloth.

Mo cut a hole in the middle.

Mo put the cloth
over his head.

"Now you are a cat,"
said Mo.
"And you are a ghost,"
said Max.

"Now we are ready for
Halloween, too!" said Mo.

Want to make a Halloween mask?

Here is what you will need:

1. A grown-up's help
2. A paper plate about nine inches across
3. Colored pencils, crayons, or paint
4. Scissors
5. One piece of paper

Here is what to do:

1. Fold

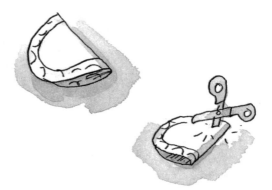

2. Poke

3. Cut

4. Cut

5. Fold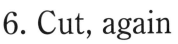

6. Cut, again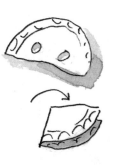

7. Tape

8. Cut

9. Tape

10. Draw and color

11. Tape